MONSTERS!

1. Auflage Mai 1999
1 - 2000

Ventil-Verlag
Augustinerstr. 18
55116 Mainz
Fon: (06131) 226078
Fax: (06131) 226079
e-Mail: ventil@exit.de
http://www.ventil-verlag.de

Layout und Satz: Jens Neumann
Lektorat und Fotos: Gunther Weinell
Covergestaltung: Mieps
Druck: Winddruck, Siegen
Bindung: Diehl, Wiesbaden

ISBN 3-930559-51-X

Reihe Popliteratur

Lee Hollis

Monsters

short-stories

Ventil-Verlag

The Author Speaks

I think I can say – with confidence and without stuttering – that, yes, this is a book. It looks like a book. It has the shape and the form of a book. It even smells like the real thing.

And that makes me happy. Because you can do a lot of things with books: You can burn them, ban them, steal them, trade them in for other books, write other books about them, sell them for MONEY ... or you can keep things traditional and just *read* them. If you *can* read, that is. Good luck!

P.S.: As always – thanks to Jens, Gunther, Mieps and ... thank you, Jesus.

Visit Lee's Web-Site:
http://www.come.to/leehollis

CONTENTS

My Name Is Hobson

My grandfather's name was Jimmie Lee Hollis. My father's name is Robert Lee Hollis, and my name is ... Hobson Lee Hollis.

H O B S O N. I don't know why they chose Hobson. Normally that's a last name. If you look in any phonebook of America, you'll find lots of Hobsons. Geraldine Hobson, Rufus Hobson, Elvis Hobson. But you will almost never find Hobson used as a first name. Hobson Presley? I don't think so. And I understand. What kind of parents would give their kid a name like that? Evil parents! I can see them now, planning my downfall ...

Mom: "Honey, I'm pregnant."

Dad: "Great! Let's call him Hobson and fuck up his childhood. Then when he grows up, he'll go on a killing rampage in some government building somewhere and then we can go on television and give interviews about how shocked we are and that he was always a good kid ..."

Mom: "... and then write a book about it and retire on some Caribbean island ..."

Dad: "... and noone will ever know that it was all planned."

Mom: "I love you, Robert Lee."

Dad: "And I love you, Jimmie Lee ..."

My parents tell me that I'm part Irish, part German (believe it or not), part something else that they couldn't remember – and all Hollis. Actually, I am the last Hollis. And if I die without having children then the whole clan will come to an end and the Hollis family will be no more. People who care about such things might say: Well, that's sad. But I don't care. My name is Hobson. H O B S O N.

To me, it sounds like the name of a butler, don't you think?

"Mmmm, Hobson, could you bring me some tea?"

"Hobson, I've got some guest coming over in about fifteen minutes, could you please clean the entire castle, cook something for around 200 people and then organize a virgin for sacrifice at midnight? Yes, some people from the church will be attending. Yes, very good, very good ..."

"Hobson, could you please wipe my ass? Yes, I didn't make it to the toilet. Thank you, Hobson, very good."

But it could be worse, I guess. I mean, they could have given me a name like, oh ... Loser.

Loser Lee Hollis. Never got picked for the basketball team:

"You, Loser! Get off the court! You, you ... loser!"

Never got a girl:

"No, I don't go out with losers."

Never got a decent job:

"I have to inform you, Mr. Hollis, that we don't hire losers."

But at least with a name like Loser you can develop some serious revenge fantasies:

"I'm no loser. Fuck you! I'll kill you!! Call me a goddamn loser and I'll make you wish you were never born ..."

But no, my name is Hobson. H O B S O N. And with a name like Hobson people just giggle. And giggling is unfortunately no good reason for murder. So I live with my name, and, like the boy called Sue, I will be stronger for it. And if I ever have a son, I'll name him Hobson Lee Hollis ... Junior. He'll grow up to be a professional wrestler, and I'll be proud of him.

Tour Diary (I)

The following is ... yes, a diary of the 17 days lasting tour in october 1998 with Jan Off and Kai Damkowski. Not the most original idea, maybe, but authentic.

That means it's all true.

No additions, corrections or over-dubs. Just me and my private, primitive thoughts and neuroses. And because they are my thoughts, I've allowed myself the power and luxury of censorship ...

I cut out the good parts.

Which only means that everything you read is true, but it's not everything. For the sad few that want to know the whole story, well ...

That costs extra. Forwards.

9. October, Mainz (100 visitors)

Wow ... That's the right way to start a tour.

Got the phone number from two sisters that I plan on sleeping with when we come to Wiesbaden. (CENSORED) is very cool.

Desperate Letter (I)

Re: Life & death

Remember the last time I had so-called "Zukunftsangst"? I sent you a long, well-written, pretty funny fax explaining that if something in my situation didn't change fast, I would end up either:

1. In jail

2. In a drug-coma in some forgotten East German hospital, or

3. In some dead-end job back in America, just another loser who "could have been somebody", but wasn't. (I think in the Ami-scenario I go on to commit suicide by throwing myself in the same boiling oil that they make the french fries in at McDonalds ...)

You were very helpful to me at that time and, if I understood you correctly, mentioned the possibility of me working for Planet Sound – or something to do with the Internet.

Kurz gesagt, es ist soweit.

Pietsch, I mostly try to maintain a positive outlook on life, but the situation I'm in at the moment is one that I've never been confronted with before and I have to say that for the first time in years – maybe the first time ever – I'm looking at the very real possibility of ... going under. Recording in America, the neu wohnung, the fucking cops from Bayern (They want 1400 marks because of this autobahn drug fiasco during the Descendants tour. Pretty fucked up, but you know what? They want 4000 from Fabsich!) and a thousand other small things have sucked away any money I thought I had.

Ich bin offiziell verzweifelt. No shit.

That's why I'm writing: In the hope that we can talk – seriously – about this Planet Sound thing ... if that's still a possibility. If not, don't worry. I'll still think you're a great guy. On the other hand, however, I am forced to ask you about this. Too many people demanding too much money – all at the same time – have pushed me into a corner that's going to be very difficult to get out of. Sure, tomorrow I'm going to our friendly Arbeitsamt to see if they have any jobs for me. At this point I'll take what I can get.

I'm desperate. And that is the whole ugly truth. Even legendary punks have to pay rent.

Tour Diary (II)

10. October, Berlin (15-20 visitors)

Fuck this city and all of the arrogant pieces of shit that live in it.

11. October, Hannover
(50 visitors with money / 25 without)

Now that's more like it. Good food (Chicken legs!), good people, and I kissed her. She's dangerous, but she kisses good ... Met the new Snob Club guitarist. Nice guy, but I guess he should get a haircut. It should always be like this.

LEE HOLLIS

Wasps

So summer's more or less now. A lot of people get romantic about summer. Just can't wait to put on those short trousers and get out and ... pray to the sun. Grab the bicycle out of the garage and thrash out 50 or 60 kilometers. Feel the burn. Be the pain. Or maybe just hang out in cafés, watching people. Yeah, summer makes most people celebrate the fact of just being alive. It's a beautiful day! You can't just sit around and watch TV! Get out and get some sun!!

I don't see it that way.

Don't get me wrong. I don't hate summer. Girls look better in the sun. If you can enjoy a good beer (and I can!), almost nothing compares to that first swallow, on a mild evening in July, with a few friends and some good-natured shit talking. So, like I said, I don't hate summer.

I just hate the sun.

And the heat.

And the sweat.

And the skin cancer.

And the ozone alerts.

But probably most of all ...

The wasps. I hate wasps. Hate 'em. I've hated them since I was a kid, and as I get older my hate only seems to grow. Wasps – are evil!

So, obviously I have a problem with wasps. I guess you could say it's almost a phobia.

Let's go back to that satisfying cold beer on a beautiful July evening. Imagine this. You're sitting there, you got your glass raised up to your lips, you're just getting ready to enjoy that first serious swallow, and then one of those yellow and black spawn of hell sits on your glass.

Now, at that point you've got a couple of choices. You can just continue to drink and accept the possibility of having a wasp in you instead of on you. In some ancient cultures this was known as "eating your enemy" and was said to be the honorable thing to do.

Or you could put your glass down, cool and sovereign, and casually swipe the little monster away. All this really does though, is piss 'em off to the point that the wasp starts to think: "Ahhh, my next victim. Ha ha ho ho!"

And that's part of the problem (okay, my problem) with wasps. You've probably heard the old cliché: "If you just leave them alone, then they won't do anything ..."

Bullshit.

A wasp can smell your fear.

When I was in school about 200 years ago, a wasp flew in and sat on my shoulder for 20 minutes or so. It was like I was his new best friend. "Hey Lee, let's go get some chicks ... buzzzzz ..."

And when I finally ran out of the classroom, screaming, he followed me.

"Lee, wait up, dude! I want to whisper something in your ear!"

They're fast, they're mean, and they don't take "no" for an answer.

A lot of people are afraid of spiders, snakes ... cockroaches ... and I can understand that, I guess. I mean – some cockroaches can fly! And in Texas they have been known to grow to about half a meter in length. I remember when my mother tried to use insect spray on one of them and he attacked her. Flew right in her face and tried to eat her eyeballs out. Luckily I had my baseball bat ready and I whacked him on the head with it. He escaped quickly, but before he left he said something like: "I will be here long after you are dead. I will feed your bones to my children! Ha ha HA!"

But normally roaches are more disgusting than dangerous. And if you're standing there in front of a spider, all you gotta do is step over – or, if you feel like it – on it. Snakes? Well, how often do you see a Python slithering through the streets of Saarbrücken?

So we're left with wasps.

And don't tell me that my fear of these little demons is illogical. Logic is only for people who need it. There's no time for logic when a wasp is involved.

I have this reoccurring dream where I'm Mike Tyson and I'm boxing against a man-sized wasp. I'm doing my best, but it's not easy boxing a wasp. I try biting his wings off and when that doesn't work I try to bite one of his antennae. Finally, in desperation, I run to my corner, grab a peanut butter sandwich and throw it at him. Of course wasps can't resist peanut butter so he attacks the sandwich and I ...

kick him between the legs ...

then I spray CS gas in his face ...

and then I eat his heart out ...

and then I look around and recognize that the audience is full of wasps.

I wake up screaming.

Why do I hate wasps so much?

I hate them because they are there.

And if you don't believe anything else I've told you, then think about this fact (and it is a fact): More people are killed by wasps every year than by shark attacks ...

So, give me a summer with cool shade, a sun tan without my skin just waiting to rot off, sweat only with a high-powered personal fan ...

... and a world without wasps. Amen.

P.S.: I have this reoccurring Clint Eastwood-, spaghetti-western-style dream in which I'm a lonesome cowboy, riding into town, just looking for a good shot of whiskey and a place to lay my head ...

I ride into Lonely Pony 'bout eight in the evening. My mouth is as dry as a Martian dust mine. I only have one thought in my sun-burned brain: Cable Television. It's Sunday night and I have an overwhelming desire to watch the Women's NBA. I park my horse and get ready to check into the local Holiday Inn when I hear a low buzzing on the street behind me. Buzzzzzzz ...!!

"What's your name, stranger?"

"Hollis. El Hollis. And what do they call you?"

"They call me Sting."

I think about it.

"You know your music sucks, don't ya?"

He just laughs:

"Ha ha ha! Hey, white boy! We have a tradition where I come from. You want to drink, you must dance with the Queen first! Ha ha ha!"

P.P.S.: And in my next wildlife report I'll explain why I hate dogs at concerts and the last two Nick Cave LPs.

Tour Diary (III)

12. October, Siegen (30 visitors)

Made a bet with Jan and lost. He's now the proud owner of my balls. Talked to Sasha for about an hour. He still likes me and that's a good thing. The "lesung" was okay, but I've got to do better. Maybe tonight ...

13. October, Frankfurt (around 40 visitors)

Finally read the nipple story ... and it worked! Feeling more relaxed with the "reading" part of the tour, thank God. Lost to Gunther (our driver and baby-sitter) playing kicker. He laughed a little too loud so I had to break his arm. Fortunately our car is an automatic, so it should be no problem ... (CENSORED)

Bubba The Slump

For about the last month I've been going through an emotional, physical and psychological slump. Now, for those of you who don't know what a "slump" is, let me explain. A slump is ... bad times. Dark days. No money, no hope, no way out. Normally I'll usually start slumping sometime during the third week of July (the start of the so-called "summer hole"), and then I'll slump into August and sometimes even on into fall. When it gets real bad I can slump even longer. My worst slump was from, I believe, September 1987 until January 1989.

When you're in a slump insult-spewing monster headaches attack you for no reason at all. I was sitting in front of my computer just recently – surfing the web – when, almost from one minute to the next, I felt a small ache in my head. I quickly put two and two together and came up with four. Nothing like a little simple mathematics to go along with unexpected pain. Then I realized that an ache in my head means I've got a headache and that my day wasn't going to get any better and that basically, basically ... I realized I was in for a fight. Because I knew that this was no normal headache.

Normal brain pain normally only shows up in the morning. And normally after a night of drinking. It's like when you get up in the morning and you know that it's your fault and you know that you'll never drink again and you know that God hates you, but at least you know why. Because you kept ordering strange and exotic drinks at outrageous prices without considering that money isn't the only way to pay for a night on the town. The day-after-headaches are hard – but fair.

Not this time. This was nothing as harmless as a hangover. It was four in the afternoon and I felt fine when I woke up this morning. No, this was a slump headache. This was war.

I turned off my computer and immediately took four aspirin which did nothing to change the state of affairs in my head, but did turn my stomach into a minefield. These days most doctors will tell you that taking aspirin is a good idea if you want to save yourself the embarrassment of having a heart attack in McDonald's, but what they don't tell you is that as soon as aspirin hit your stomach they start acting like American soldiers in Vietnam ...

"We're gonna have to napalm that wall over there. I need a couple of volunteers for a suicide mission."

Aspirin don't know the difference between right and wrong; they only know that they have a job to do.

"Jawohl!" they screamed and started bombing the inside of my belly.

At the same time my pain-killers were causing me so much pain that my slump – whom I'll call "Bubba" – could go to work on the rest of my body.

"Yeah, you feel like shit, don't ya?" he asked me.

My headache, which had started at the base of my skull, was now slowly crawling up and around the left side of my head, which by now was starting to feel like the inside of a bowling alley. A sports announcer in my brain started to give me the play-by-play ...

"Ladies and gentlemen, you can feel the tension here in the room as Doug Dickson lines up his shot ..."

Of course he was right. I could feel the tension.

"Doug is taking his time. He needs a strike to advance to the finals. You can feel the tension ..."

"The tension, the tension," I thought, "I can feel it ..."

"Standing behind Doug is his arch rival Dick Dougson. He's looking pretty tense himself. You can almost feel it ..."

"I feel it! I feel it! Now, would you please shut up?!"

"Doug is going into his delivery. It's looking good ... looking good ... YES! A perfect strike! Doug Dickson has done it again! He is in the finals!! Wait, what's this? Dick Dougson does not look happy! He's got his bowling ball in his hand ... Oh my Good Lord! Dick Dougson has just cracked Doug Dickson's head wide open with his ball!! My God, you can absolutely feel the tension here tonight ...!"

"I think maybe I should lay down," I thought to myself and tried to stand up. Bubba the slump, however, had other ideas.

"Just a minute there, young man ... And where do you think you're going?" he asked me.

"To bed. Like I said. Doug is a dick."

"No no no, you don't understand. Doug has made it into the finals. That means he's going to bowl again. It could take hours." Then he laughed, as any self-respecting slump would: "Ha ha ha HO HA!"

I fell to my knees and started crawling toward my bedroom. I noticed that the floor hadn't been cleaned for weeks. I rolled over on my back and looked at the ceiling. Also dirty. Sooo dirty. I stayed that way, on my back, studying the ceiling for, what – two minutes? Two hours? Who knows! Time ignored me.

"Are you going to stay down there all day?"

What?! Who said that?

"It's me, Bubba."

"Who?" I asked, barely able to open my eyes.

"Bubba, your slump. Get up!"

"Fuck you, Bubba. This is my floor and I'll lie on it as long as I want to."

"No, Lee, you don't understand. You have to get up. It's important."

I rolled over on my stomach and tried to stand so that I could see who I was talking to. I didn't make it. Instead I ended up face-down on the floor, with my arms spread out at right angles around me. I looked like Jesus on the cross, only someone had forgotten to plant me in the ground. I moaned.

"Why me, Lord? Why?" I asked the floor.

Bubba had the answer.

"Because it's your turn. You're on the list."

Bubba pulled out a small digital personal organizer and "beeped" it on.

"Beep!"

"Here," he said, "right here, see? Hollis, Hobson Lee – Standard."

"Standard?" I asked.

"Standard means you don't die. You only suffer."

"Why?"

"Wrong question, friend. 'Why not?' would be better. Everybody's on the list. It just happens to be your turn. Now, can we stop bullshitting? You have to stand up. We have a lot to do and not much time ..."

I started crying.

"What list? Who are you? And why do I have to stand up?"

Bubba smiled a thin, evil smile.

"Because you have to answer the door. You have guest."

At that moment the doorbell rang – and my head exploded. The bowling alley in my brain had somehow transformed itself into a hidden nuclear testing site. Probably planted there by CIA agents, I thought.

After I had finished screaming and begging my doorbell for mercy I gathered together the last bit of strength I had and crawled to answer the door. Feeling very much like some "undead" thing in a zombie film and still on my knees, I reached up, turned the doorknob, ripped the door open and ...

CIA agents. Or at least what looked like CIA agents. Two men in black suits, mirror sunglasses, carrying black leather bags, stepped over my dying body and into my apartment. I tried to speak to them.

"Uuuugh, uh ..."

While one of them started making calls on a cellular phone, the other one knelt in front of me and pulled out a business card. I tried to read it but I couldn't keep my eyes focused, so the first agent read it for me.

"The name's Dickson. Doug Dickson. This is my partner Dougson. Dick Dougson."

"Wha ...?"

"You're probably wondering what we're doing here."

I was, actually. I figured that the way my day was developing, he'd probably say something insane like – they'd come to bowl in my hallway ...

"We've come to bowl, Mr. Hollis – in your hallway."

It was – to put it lightly – all too much for me. In the words of two famous cartoon characters: it sucked. All these strange people, strange voices ... bowling. Listen, I try to be a nice guy. Really, I do. But there are limits to how nice a guy can be when you've got people you don't know in your home, setting up bowling pins, polishing their balls and yelling "strike!" right next to your face. It was time for action. It was time for ... the slump gun.

I crawled into my bedroom, thinking that if this really was the end, then I was going to end it on my terms, not those of government bowling agents. I looked under my bed and there, right next to my cat — also named Bubba – there it was: my slump gun. Manufactured in Brazil and banned in most parts of the developed world, only twenty of these pieces of destructive art have ever been built. I had to sign a piece of paper saying that I would never reveal how it works, so you'll have to use your imagination. But believe me: It works. I think Arnold Schwarzenegger has one. I hear that Bill Gates also has one, but he doesn't know how to use it. I know that Nixon had one 'cause he told me. And I've got one. And it was loaded.

I put on my mirror sunglasses and crawled back into the hallway which by now was filled with people. Cameramen, bowling fans of all shapes and sizes. I noticed Dick Dougson giving an interview to some hot-shot reporter from "Weird Sports":

"You see, bowling isn't just a sport. It's a way of life. Why, I sleep with my balls ..."

I got to my feet, staggered into the kitchen and found Bubba wearing a (what else?) pink and black bowling shirt with "Betty's Garage" printed on the back. I stuck my slump gun in his ear and said: "Bubba, can I borrow your digital organizer for a second?"

Bubba, probably too shocked to speak, took out his organizer and handed it to me.

"Thanks. Now let me see ... Batman, Briggs, Bank Of America ... Bubba the cat, Bubba the auto mechanic, Bubba the hair-dresser ... Bubba the Slump! Hey dude, you're also on the list! What a surprise!"

Bubba looked nervous.

"And you know what else? It doesn't say Standard!!"

Bubba started to whimper.

"You know what it says, Bubba, old friend?!"

Bubba started to cry and beg for mercy.

"If I'm reading this correctly, it says Total! Total destruction! TOTAL!!!"

Some people will tell you that wanting revenge is an example of human nature at its most primitive. They'll try to explain that understanding and forgiving are the best ways to handle situations like this. They'll say that the act of revenge only leads to more violence, more chaos and more pain. Some people – are full of shit. Revenge is COOL! It's fun! It should be an Olympic sport! One pump of the slump gun and I had Bubba all over my kitchen, but the look in his eyes alone was worth the time I spent cleaning up. In fact it was so much fun that I didn't even stop there. And you know what? I didn't know that you can use a slump gun on a bowler – but you can.

Tour Diary (IV)

14. October, Köln (30 visitors)

Small, but nice. Met some Spermbirds fans. At least they are ready for the reunion ... Me too, to tell the truth. Jan became an uncle. He's a good guy. Kai left us today. Echt schade. Met a nice girl named Birgit and had beer and pickles for breakfast at a place complete with ugly old men with powerdrills. It was hell.

15. October, Heidelberg (45-50 visitors)

Lesung – good. I'm getting better. Our promoter – a little shit-talking so-called "anarchist" parasite.

"You've got a lot to learn," I told him at one point.

Jan continues to impress me. He said that being on tour with me is like moving up to a different league. (I'd hate to see the places he normally reads) Talked to Maria for a long time. It surprises me how much people I know here in Germany. And yes, I am thankful.

Call Me Conservative

There's no real good reason for me to tell you this, but it is a true story. And I'll never forget it ... I was sitting in a diner at about one in the morning, eating scrambled eggs and toast, when an old drunk asked me the following question:

"You know what a freak is?"

Here it comes, I thought. He's gonna insult me. This pea-brain, drunk, piece of shit has decided to harass me because I'm dressed funny. (I was dressed kind of funny. Mom's clothes ...)

Before I could react my new friend decided to explain it to me.

"A freak is when you take a baby – don't matter if it's a boy or a girl – you take 'em ... and you cut 'em – from the asshole right up to the throat. Then you let 'em bleed. After they finished bleedin', what's left is a freak ..."

I was eating eggs. I think I even pointed at my eggs, as if to say: I know you're a sick motherfucker, but I'm eating. But he didn't recognize my sign language. He just turned to one of his drunk friends and they laughed about how clever he was. I left. Call me conservative ...

Tour Diary (V)

16. October, Wiesbaden (Lots of people)

Felt like Hunter Thompson with his attorney. Took many drugs legal and otherwise, talked to many people, smoked at least two and a half packs of cigarettes and generally acted like your average speed freak. A nice guy from Sweden asked Jan if he knew where he could get some more water. But Jan wasn't interested in water.

"No, motherfucker! Do you know where we can get some fucking cocaine?!"

Puked in a plastic bag in the car most of the day, but once again – I survived.

Thank you, Jesus.

HOLLIS

The Golf War

I was sitting in a van, driving to a concert a few weeks ago, and I was staring out of the window when within one hour we were passed by three Volkswagens ... a Golf Bon Jovi, a Golf Rolling Stones and a Golf Pink Floyd. It was really kind of scary.

I mean, you've got to wonder what kind of people actually pay money for these cars. I've been a fan, I guess, of Nick Cave's for years, but I wouldn't want his name on my car (especially after his last two records). As a matter of fact the only name I would have on my car would be mine ... Jaguar Lee Hollis. 63 Mustang ... Lee Hollis. Top fuel dragster ... Lee Hollis. I could live with that. But please God, not Genesis. You might as well just hang a sign on the door that says:

"I have no taste or style what-so-ever. I am the reason why Phil Collins continues to make money with third class pop songs. I am damaged. Please kill me and stop my suffering."

So I tried to imagine a young couple going to their local Volkswagen dealer and picking out their new set of wheels:

"See honey, I told you they don't have the Spice Girls."

"And I believed you, sweetheart. But I was sure that they had Michael Jackson ..."

"Didn't you read about them having Tina Turner?"

"Yeah, but they're waiting for her new record to be released. Listen, let's just get the Genesis and get it over with."

"Oh okay, which one? The purple or the neon green ...?"

The young couple buys the purple Golf de Genesis because it matches his suit. And they both drive around happily listening to Genesis all day, only to die in a head-on collision with a Ferrari de Steakknife ... which is fair.

But that's not the point. Corporate sponsorship of Rock'n'Roll is nothing new these days, and if The Who are getting 20 millions from Marlboro – why should anybody really care?

It just continues to amaze me that there are people – and a lot of them by the look of things – who truly think that it's cool to have Bon Jovi on the side of their Golf. And the whole thing is so alien to me that I start to fantasize about how these folks live. What do their houses look like? What do they talk about? For example:

"Honey, where are you going?"

"I'm going to the toilet Jethro Tull."

"You know we don't have any toilet paper Guns'n'Roses."

"Oh, that's okay. I'll just use my hands ... What's for dinner tonight?"

"I thought I'd make, uh ... Meatloaf."

He goes to the toilet and comes back with shit all over his hands.

"Dear, I'm not feeling too good. Have you seen my shotgun Nirvana?"

"It's behind the refrigerator Ice Cube."

He grabs his gun and ... kills his whole family.

So obviously these people are dangerous, and I personally have decided that I'm not going to just stand by and let it happen. No, I'm going to war.

The Golf war.

And I've got some men outside in the parking lot checking to see what kind of cars you people drive, and I'm checking to see if any of you have shit on your hands ... or shotguns hanging out of your mouths.

So think seriously before you buy your next car. Think about the consequences. Think about life – and death. And pray that you make the right choice – 'cause if it continues at the pace it's going, then the day might come that Volkswagen will be building our rock stars for us (folk rock stars, he he ...). I can already see the advertisement:

"The year is 2020 – the year Volkswagen reinvented Rock. Ladies & gentlemen, put your hands together for the one and only rock star you will ever need! He's lean! He's mean! A little man – a lot of machine! Part car – part guitar!! Brothers and sisters ... !!! ... The new Golf."

(First published in Testcard #5 "Kulturindustrie – Wissen für den Dancefloor", Mainz 1998)

Tour Diary (VI)

17. October, Wolfsburg (6 people maybe ... ?)

After a day of living hell in the car we got there and read for five of Jan's friends (nice folks, by the way). It was like a campfire thing and just what I needed at that point. I think Jan experienced his first dose of "tour stress". After two days of excess he snapped at little and got mad at Gunther for reasons still unknown. I tried to smooth things over and nobody died, but I'm hoping it was a one-time occurance. We can't control assholes from the outside (Okay, we could simply kill them, but then we'd have lots of paper work to deal with), but I won't accept stress from the inside. It became very quickly very clear to me that, as much as I like Jan, I would have to send him home if he can't control himself. But I'm sure he can ...

I hope.

Confession Of A Cramps Fan

"The only reason they're so popular is because they're old ..." was what the guy told me, and for a second I thought I had misunderstood him.

"Uh, could you repeat that please?" I asked.

He could.

"They are old, boring, they have no relevance in a modern society and – did I forget to mention that they're very o-l-d?"

I looked at the guy. A young guy whom I normally credited with having pretty good taste – and a friend of mine. Mieps sold t-shirts for Steakknife for about two years until graduating to guitar a few months ago. He has experienced the ups and downs of being stuffed in a bus with five or six other sweaty, dirty, whining men for two or three weeks at a time, and I thought that he'd handled the whole ugly process pretty good.

Until now.

Be careful Lee, I thought to myself. Remember,

he's your friend. He's normally a good guy. You don't have to hurt him. It doesn't have to end this way. Maybe he's just having a bad day. Or bad drugs. Or ... or ...

But no.

Mieps knew exactly what he was talking about. And by the way he spoke I could tell that he was serious. I fingered the butterfly knife in my pocket, wondering if I should cut his tongue out first and maybe wave it in front of his face while saying something like "Bad boy. Bad boy!" or if I should just go directly for the throat instead and keep his suffering at a minimum. He was, after all, my friend.

I decided to give him one more chance.

"Mieps," I said, "you can only hope that you have that much energy and style when you hit 51."

He just laughed, and in that moment I knew that he would have to die.

First you need to understand why I'm such a big Cramps fan.

During the early eighties there were probably three bands that influenced me more than any other.

First, The Birthday Party because they were the only ones to successfully reproduce the sound of elephants fucking on vinyl. Listen to the song

"Swampland" on the "Mutiny" ep from '84 and you'll understand what I'm talking about.

Second, Minor Threat because "Oh, don't those guys play fast?!" In fact, they played so fast and so good that I can almost forgive them for accidentally starting a fascist religion (Straight Edge) and destroying the lives of young men all over the world. (By the way, I wonder why it's mostly guys – boys – who feel the need to unite under some kind of flag of purity and sexlessness. Are women truly the more intelligent species? Kinda creepy when you think about it.)

And finally, The Cramps because they were (and still are!) so fucking cool and truly strange.

I see it like this: Marilyn Manson obviously wants you to believe that he's weird and dangerous, and it looks like he spends a shitload of money on his videos trying to achieve that effect.

The Cramps could go on stage wearing jogging suits, with their hair in curlers, playing an old acoustic guitar with two strings and a trashcan, and still be more threatening than Mrs. Manson. And, furthermore, Lux Interior has more humor in his little finger than Manson has in his whole zit-covered body.

Excuse my passion, but we're talking about two different leagues here: The difference between a

Pentium III on 450 MHz and an old 286 that you couldn't give away.

We're talking about – the basics. Leaders and followers. Innovators and imitators.

Why didn't Mieps understand this? Why? And what could I do to help him?

The answer was simple. Nothing. Not one thing. In spite of our friendship we had reached a black and white area. No grey tones allowed. It hurt me to know that I would have to hurt him, but it was too late.

"Mieps, come here," I said.

Tour Diary (VII)

18. October, Greifswald (15-20?)

The EAST. Not easy. Jan didn't read because he's not professional. I did, but I had to ask myself: Do these people even know what the hell I'm talking about? As it turns out they did, but laughter doesn't come easy in the ex-DDR, so I struggled. Had breakfast with two nice young ladies ... Ahh, the girl with the dreads. Almost difficult saying goodbye – but fun ...

By the way: Some friendly young people (including my new dreadlocked sweetheart) came too late for the reading and waited for my second set. I almost felt guilty, but I had to tell them that I don't do second sets. Maybe I'll come back in the summer – probably not, but God ... she was, well, young for one thing. (CENSORED) Hell, you know what I mean ...

Satan

She was a good-natured, nice young lady – it was just that when she turned her head around, you could hear her spine crack ...

My first girlfriend's name was Amy Wakefield – but that's not what I want to tell you about. I'd like to talk about Satan. Satan and one of the darkest summers of my life. A summer when the shadows were darker, the nights longer, and even the days seemed to be losing the battle against evil. The summer fear became my constant companion.

Like many kids young and old I was fascinated – but not particularly horrified – by horror films. And after being fed the best (and worst) of what the 70's splatter masters could offer, I thought that, at the ripe old age of 13, I had seen it all. The 'Omen' films didn't bother me – except when the kid smiles at the end of the first one ...

I laughed at 'Dawn of the Dead'. I still do, actually. For some reason I find scenes of people being eaten alive, uh ... funny. Doesn't everybody?

Okay, 'Friday the 13th' made me a little nervous, but only because the guy at school who kept threatening to cut my throat because he thought I was ugly was also named Jason.

'The Exorcist', though, was a different situation. I didn't actually see the film until years later, but after Amy's sister had described all the pea-puking, head-twisting, crucifix-fucking details to me even going to baseball practise became a test of nerves.

Lucifer knew where I lived, and my soul belonged to him.

I was sitting with Amy in her parent's kitchen when her sister Judy came in. Jude was at the end of 17 and living life in the fast-lane 70's style. Lynyrd Skynyrd were at the height of their popularity and kids were running away from home in record numbers, supposedly because of their bombastic hit 'Free bird'. "Lord knows I can't change" was thc suspected lyric that caused all the breakouts, and God knows we couldn't.

Jude hadn't run away yet - she would never get the chance - but she was doing her best to rebel against "the man" with the few tools available to her. Lite-beer hadn't been invented yet, but whiskey-drinking had been around since the beginning of time, and pot-smoking even longer. Stuck somewhere between Hippie and hatred, she was, in short, a teenage wreck.

She died 2 years later trying to cover up an affair with one of the local minorities. It seems there were complications involving a coat-hanger and an unwanted child. Inter-racial dating, much less fucking, was still frowned upon in North Carolina at that time.

On this night, however, she had just come home from the movies. Jude had been trying to convince Amy and I that the only good kiss was a french kiss. I was still kinda new at this kissing thing and found the idea of sticking my tongue in someone's mouth – to use a phrase from back then – "yucky". Amy felt the same way, and we both decided that, no matter what Jude said, there was no way we would "swap slobber" during our teenage attempts at kissing.

But Jude was sure we would love it.

"I'll leave the room for a few minutes, you two kiss like I told you, then I'll come back and we'll talk about it, okay?"

Amy and I looked at each other and we told Jude that we would try. Jude was almost out of the room, when *that* song came on the radio. 'Tubular Bells'. The theme song from *that* film.

"Isn't that the music from 'The Exorcist'?" I asked.

"Hell yeah, it is!" said Jude, full of enthusiasm. "That's the movie we saw tonight. Fuckin' great movie!" and proceeded to act out a few of the more graphic scenes for our entertainment. She made herself puke on the floor and started throwing the result 'round the kitchen. She grabbed the cross hanging over the sink and fucked herself bloody for about five or six minutes, screaming obscenities in latin and babbling backwards the whole time. She must have gotten her films confused, 'cause then she crawled over to Amy and began chewing on her leg, which in turn began bleeding. Amy turned to me and smiled ...

As you can imagine, this was all making me pretty nervous, but I was doing my best to keep my 13-year-old self under control.

"Everything okay, Jude?" I asked, trying to be helpful.

"Great!" she screamed, "Everything's fuckin' GREAT!" and went back to what was left of Amy's leg. Amy herself was slouched down on her chair, her head hanging to one side. I couldn't make out what, but she seemed to be – singing.

By this time the kitchen was awash with puke, blood and whiskey from a bottle that decided that it was the right moment to fly across the room and explode right behind my head. Upon hearing the explosion, Jude looked up from her meal and at me. I don't know if she actually saw me 'cause her eyes had rolled back in her head, but she was grinning.

"Come here, Lee. Let me show you how grown-ups kiss," she hissed as she tried to stand up.

At the same moment Amy seemed to wake up out of her trance. She stopped singing and spoke to her sister.

"No way, Jude. He's my boyfriend, and anyway, I'm tired of you always flirting with the men I bring home."

"This is flirting?" I thought to myself – I'd hate to see her fighting ...

"Shut up, bitch," she said, "the virgin belongs to me ..."

"The virgin?" I thought. And then: "Oh yeah, she's right ..."

"My virgin!" replied Amy. "Tell us about the rest of the movie."

Anything to keep me from being eaten.

"Yeah, Jude. What happened then?" I asked.

Jude was, if anything, an entertainer.

"Well, one of the coolest scenes is when Regan – that's the possessed girl's name – Regan twists her head around so that she's facing backwards. It was so cool!"

Jude then held her arms out in front of her, zombie-like, and gave us a demonstration.

As her head slowly rotated to the left, the sound coming out of her mouth was a cross between a didgeridoo and a train at full speed with the breaks on. The kind of noise that had the potential to be a dancefloor-hit if the right DJ got his hands on it. The sound coming from her back, however, was the very realistic pop-crack-pop of her spine snapping ...

I woke up in my bed the next day. The sun was up and I could hear my parents going through their morning routine downstairs. Honestly confused, I walked downstairs to see what had happened.

It was Sunday, and my father was getting ready for an afternoon of American football by drinking the first of many beers.

"Hey Lee," said my mother, "you fell asleep at Amy's last night. Her parents drove you home. Want breakfast?"

Fell asleep???

"What about Amy's leg?" I asked.

"Well, what about it ...?"

Bill Cosby once said that, as a child, monsters live in your bedroom closet. I'd say: Not only in your closet, and not only as a child ...

Tour Diary (VIII)

19. October, Jena (50-60)

The biggest surprise on the tour so far. I was expecting, at the most, 15 people, probably skinheads with hate in their hearts. We arrive late and walk into ... a packed house (Okay, it's not the biggest house in the world, but full). The last thing I was expecting. And they listened, they laughed at the right places – God, I think I'll move here. No shit. Jena is cool. Pretty city, trees everywhere and a beautiful young woman on every corner. A small pearl in a mostly grey East Germany. My "insider tip" for the writer on the road. Amen.

The Nipple Incident

"We got a problem with your buttons," said Mr. Peniski, leaning over my shoulder. Sasha Peniski was my boss or, as I liked to call him, my "contact person" and probably one of the first yuppies I had ever seen live.

"What's the problem?" I asked. I had made the buttons about 2 months before and it irritated me that it took them that long to decide that they weren't up to standards.

"They look like nipples."

Nipples.

Now, I'd be the first to admit that nipples can be a problem sometimes. There is no pain that can compare to having your tongue caught in some young woman's freshly pierced ... whatever. But I was proud of my buttons, and accusing them of mascarading as nipples had as much logic as saying that an american football is in reality an entire breast.

I turned to Peniski and repeated his opinion.

"Nipples?"

"Yeah, nipples."

I actually thought they looked like nice, tiny pink & white marshmellows.

The pornographic buttons in question weren't made for a shirt or jeans, but for the internet.

And my job?

Internet web page design.

Sounds almost sexy, doesn't it?

WEB PAGE DESIGN.

The new Hip Hop. Bad-ass boys (and girls of course), dressed in black, designing bad-ass web-sites for dumb-ass businessmen who don't even know why they need them, but they need them NOW.

Although I do wear black, I'm not a very good bad-ass and I didn't even really want the job – only the money. So there I was: designing nippl... uh buttons for people who were – in every sense of the word – yuppie scum.

"Are you sure?"

Peniski was sure.

"I'm sure," he said, "Change them."

So I did. And as I was de-nipplizing my buttons I thought about Peniski. Poor guy. He must live in constant terror of anything even remotely sexual. Or maybe even worse: Everything was sexual, and he spent his day stumbling from one imagined orgy to the next. 24 hours a day.

Then it occurred to me that Peniski had said "We have a problem ..." and not "I have a problem ...". That could only mean that there was not one, but two sex-possessed yuppies involved here. And I knew who the second one was: Rudy, Peniski's business partner. I don't have too much bad to say about Rudy. He was always pretty nice to me, but he did spend a lot of time in the toilet ...

Feeling more than a little paranoid, I checked to see if anybody was watching me, remembering in the last second to put out my cigarette. God knows what would happen if they saw me with a finger-shaped object hanging out of my mouth.

Nobody was watching, so I went back to my buttons.

About thirty minutes later Peniski came back and inspected my buttons.

"No no NO!" he exclaimed, getting louder with each shrill "NO!".

"What's the problem now?" I asked.

Peniski looked at me with true anger in his eyes.

"Do you even know what these buttons are for?!"

I could see that he was very close to exploding. Some people get very emotional about their buttons.

"Uh, for the internet?" I offered.

"You don't understand anything!" answered Peniski, even louder now, and started pacing around the room, holding his forehead as if a monster headache had just ambushed his little peabrain.

At that moment the situation became clear to me. Welcome to office politics. This is how the business world communicates. Forget the internet – Peniski's logic was that if he screamed at me, I'd get nervous and start begging for forgiveness ... anything to keep my job and make the boss happy. I looked at my buttons – which now looked like bananas – and tried to keep the situation from escalating.

"But Peniski, I changed them like you wanted ...," but he cut me off. He was sweating now and kinda reminded me of a volcano waiting for the right time to erupt.

"You understand NOTHING!" he screamed again and threw some papers around the room.

At first I wanted to stay cool. I wanted to do the right thing. But the last time someone yelled at me like that was in the army. I didn't like it then, and at that moment it occurred to me that I still didn't like it.

And anyway, what Sasha didn't know was that screaming is my job.

"Uh, Mr. Peniski ...?"

Sounds of broken glass, more shrieks and cursing ...

"Sasha ..."

Someone calling the police. Rudy's feet running down the hallway to where we were standing. Peniski, now directly in front of me, face tomato-red, animal noises and spit pouring out of his mouth ...

"Stop screaming at me!!" I screamed.

And, for a split-second, he did stop. His eyes were moving independently of each other and his hands clinched into fists. He looked truly dangerous.

Seeing my chance to take control of the situation, I grabbed him by the nipples and started swinging him around the room.

He howled. He foamed at the mouth. He prayed to some obscene god ...

He liked it.

At that moment Rudy came.

"What the hell is going on here?" he asked.

"Hey Rudy!" I said, still spinning Peniski around the office, "How's it hanging, baby? Want to nipple-dance with us? Here, catch!"

I then swung Sasha in Rudy's direction, who just missed catching Peniski before he went diving out of the fifth floor window Rudy was standing beside. For a short moment there was silence.

Rudy and I stood motionless, looking at each other. Pieces of paper floated like confetti through the room. I shrugged my shoulders.

"I thought you would catch him ...," I said.

Rudy looked out of the window and then back at me. After a few seconds in which he seemed to be thinking, he shrugged his shoulders.

"You're fired," he said and then dived out the window after Sasha.

Tour Diary (IX)

20. October, Gera (25)

We asked for schnitzel and we got it! Jan had a great reading. He was good and they loved him. I didn't have as much luck. There seemed to be a serious language barrier (Or maybe I simply sucked ... naaaah) and I spit in the microphone and killed the P.A. Pretty cool when you think about it. Destroying speakers just by reading ... Man, I am so hard.

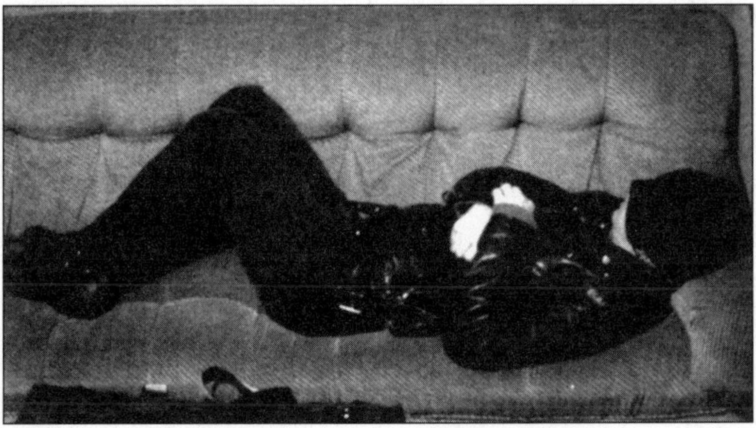

Two Last Puke Stories

I.

I was walking home around two in the afternoon, on a truly beautiful day in March, when I saw a kid about 17-18 who seemed to have problems walking. I suspected that alcohol was involved and watched him for a while. After a few unsuccessful attempts at mobility, he finally accepted his situation and decided to test standing still.

Several different scenarios flashed through my head: Critical System Error. Not Enough Memory.

He might have ended up face down on hard city concrete, were it not for the church. Instead of breaking his nose on the pavement, he simply found God and cracked his head open on the wall of a small, almost cute church in the middle of wanna-be city, Saarbrücken. I guess I knew what was going to happen next, so I walked over and started talking to him.

"Are you okay?"

He starts puking.

"No, you're not okay, are you?"

He continues puking.

"You're a dumb motherfucker who can't handle his alcohol, aren't you?"

He tries to talk, but is interrupted by the continuing flow of vomit.

"Dumb motherfucker ... This is one day you'll never forget, boy. One day you'll look at your children and wonder why you hate them so much, and then you'll remember today and realize that it's 'cause they're dumb motherfuckers, just like you. It's fate. You can't fight it."

More puking. I start to laugh.

"Wait, I got to get a picture of this. I need a document."

I pull out my camera and take a photo. He's puking through his nose now.

"You think you hate yourself now? Wait 'til you wake up tomorrow. That's when the party really starts ..."

I laugh really loud and take another photo.

"Stupid shit."

He continues puking and I continue laughing ...

II.

A friend of mine puked in three different corners of the same bar, on the same night. Fucking hero, if you ask me ...

Tour Diary (X)

21. October, Leipzig (25)

Strange. Guess I'm not the superstar I thought I was. I truly expected more people. Fuck it. Could be wrong, but I thought I read – well, verdammt good. Crisp, direct, wide-awake. Schwapp came. We exchanged news and smoked some of his nuclear grass. Wow. Seriously stoned. The cops stopped us on the way to some reggae club. I thought we were finished. Gunther took an alcohol test, and just as I was getting ready for a full body search – they let us go. My relief was physical. Got to the club – located under a prison ... an ugly prison – and drooled over a group of 15-year-old girls that I would have paid money for to see naked. Amazing. So sexy, so young has to be criminal ... Oh yeah, it is criminal. Got to the place we were sleeping at and bullshitted with Jan for a few hours. We both agreed that East Germany's not really Germany. The people are simply different. Their humor, their logic, their so-called "way of life". They laugh at things that aren't meant to be funny, and their timing is bad. I have the fee-

ling that they don't really trust us. That's okay though, 'cause I don't really trust them either.

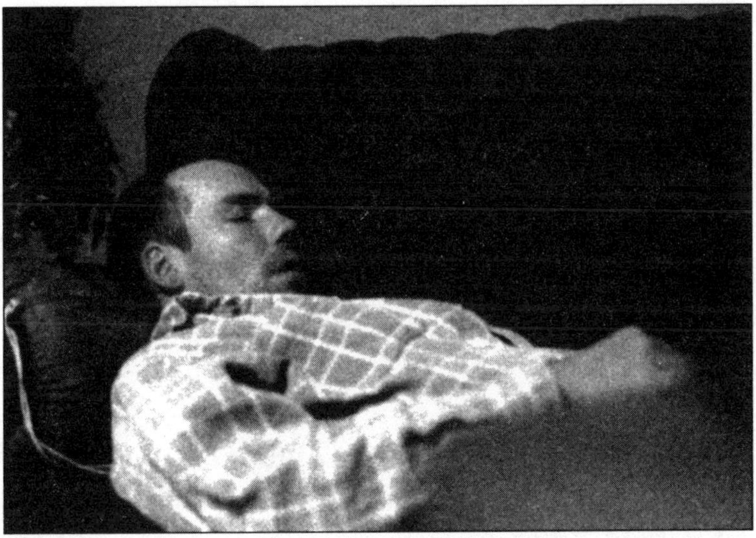

Going Home

Going home. Make yourself at home. Feel at home. Home sweet home. Home is where your heart is. My home is my castle. Home run. Homing device. Home, where my love lies waiting silently for me ... Right.

Having been living as an American in Germany for over ten years (fifteen, counting the time spent as a paid killer in Kaiserslautern), I was excited and more than a little nervous about going back to America for the first time in over half a decade. Would I fly into San Francisco, get off the plane and realize that, yes, I am an American and this is my country and all of these people running around talking too fast are indeed my people? Or would they grab me at customs and drag me chained and screaming into a small room with no windows, one naked light bulb and a dripping sink where Bubba and Slim would beat me with rubber rods and ask me about some ugly night in Texas with the one-legged cowboy and a suitcase full of money all those years ago ...

My question was: Would I feel at home? I talked to my therapist about it, a Greek whose name I can't divulge for legal reasons ...

"You have no feelings for the country where you were born?"

"Of course I have. Fear. Hate. Intense paranoia."

The Greek sat back and thought.

"Hmmm, I'm going to write you a prescription for some pills called Taxilan. Take one in the morning, one at night, and with any luck you'll sleep through the whole experience."

Sounded good to me.

"And what about side effects?" I asked him.

"Others than the possible loss of your reproductive organs, your eyesight and a total breakdown of your nervous system – none. I would advise against mixing them with alcohol ..."

He then told me a story about an ex-patient of his who, after mixing Taxilan with cheap beer and bad speed, stripped his clothes off, ran screaming into a nearby Burger King and demanded that "The Whopper" be changed to "The Whimper" because – well, just because. But it was Monday and the girl behind the cash register wasn't about to take any shit from some insane and probably dangerous Taxilan addict ... so she shot him.

I thought this was all pretty cool. I took the prescription, bought the pills, immediately mixed them with alcohol and got on the plane.

After a twelve-hours-flight I woke up to find myself in the country where I was born. In a country where a fat sex-fiend who "jogs to forget" called Clinton is "the Boss". Where a typical night on television starts with "The World's Most Deadly Natural Disasters", then moves on to "The World's Most Disgusting Car Crashes", followed by "The World's Most Dangerous Animals" (featuring a rabid house cat that eats a woman's leg live on camera!), right before two "real crime" series, "Cops" and "LAPD", all topped off with "The Nightly News" (8 dead in freak car accident! 17 massacred in gang violence! 35 lost in industrial explosion! 100s missing after earthquake!! 1000s dying right next door to where YOU LIVE!!!). It's no wonder most Americans live in constant fear. Armageddon isn't just around the corner. It's happening now, as we speak. Don't you watch TV?

I got off the plane, made it through customs and took an airport shuttle to my hotel in downtown San Francisco (Waterbeds! Cable TV! Pornography!!). On the way over the shuttle driver explained to me that "driving was his life", as I sat and watched my country zip by through the window. I recognized two things pretty quickly: There are more cars in America – and more signs. Signs everywhere, all advertising the key to true happiness and ultimate fulfillment.

"Hemorrhoids acting up again? Kill the fuckers with new, improved Hem-away!"

"Guns?! We got guns! We got assault rifles! Insult rifles!! Shot guns! Grease guns! Gas guns! Just jump into one of your cars and head on over to Gary's Gun Shack, where our motto is: There's no problem so big that you can't shoot the shit out of it!"

And of course signs promising a better sex life if you would only buy a Chevy instead of some plastic Jap piece of shit.

I got to my hotel and immediately started making phonecalls. I called my lawyer in New York and told him to sue my lawyer in Los Angeles. I called my accountant in Nashville and told him to start counting the money I received from my agent in Berlin. I called my therapist in Saarbrücken and told him to send more Taxilan. I called the room-service and told them to send up a case of Mexican beer, a bag full of limes, two nuclear burritos from "Billy's Burrito Bordello" and an elephant rifle with a high-powered infra-red scope for what we in the business call "night work".

Then I went exploring.

If you're ever walking around in downtown San Francisco let me give you a few tips. Never look anyone in the eye. Stay away from people buying and selling crack. And don't use the public toilets. There's always a long line to wait in, and the minute you set foot in one of those things everybody in the line just knows you're injecting some sort of illegal substance into your body. I was sitting there – doing my business – when the woman next in line started yelling at me to "Get the fuck outta there you fucking junky!"

Of course I knew she was wrong because I was only taking Taxilan and I had a prescription that was totally legal in most states.

"Go fuck yourself!" I screamed back. Sitting on the toilet always makes me feel primitive. I finished what I was doing and stormed out of the cubicle to find that the lady who was giving me a hard time was sitting in a wheelchair. I thought about letting the air out of her tires ... Naw, the hell with it. Abusing invalids isn't one of my hobbies – anymore.

"I need more food," I thought to myself and found a Chinese/American diner complete with red leather booths just like the ones you see in gangster movies, and Chinese people making the food. I thought back to all the John Woo films I had seen and checked the exits. One, two. Gonna have to be good enough. I mean, I was hungry, but you never know when some insane Chinese fry-cook is gonna decide to start machine-gunning you into little pieces in slow-motion only because he doesn't like your face. I sat down and ordered two eggs, over-easy with sausage, toast and a Bloody-Mary.

As I waited for my food, I looked out the window and watched humanity stumble by. Businessmen, beautiful Asian women, a guy with no legs and an old acoustic guitar singing a song I believe was called "Helpless" ... On the other corner a young kid, obviously retarded, doing his best to beg for money – unsuccessfully.

As a white limousine drove by I remembered reading in a local music magazine that Tom Petty would be playing an entire week at the Fillmore, starting the very next day. I stroked my elephant rifle seductively, thinking that maybe I should go visit old crazy Tom. Just crash into his backstage room guns blazing, with me spitting and spewing hatred and chaos in all directions ...

"You reap what you sow, Tommy-Boy! YOU REAP WHAT YOU SOW!! YOU SHOULD HAVE SHAVED THIS MORNING!!!"

Which only means Petty deserves to die and that I would be doing him a favor by splattering his fucking hippie brain all over the wall. He would understand – and thank me ...

But I had no time for such attractive diversions. I was looking for "home", and anyway, the rifle was only for my personal protection, not for "cowboy-justice" fantasies. As Mom would say: "It's not a toy, Lee. You'll go blind."

I finished my eggs, drank my Bloody-Mary, paid (tipped good) and left. After passing the usual pawn-shops and porno-emporiums, I walked up to – and into – one of the the largest shopping malls I personally have ever seen. Something like twenty stories high. Twenty stories filled with the American Dream in its purest form: shopping. I looked down at my shoes ... and decided that I had come to the right place. Home or not, if you want to spend money mindlessly, America is arguably the best place on the planet to do it. But I wanted to start at the top, so I did. I took the elevator up to the twenty-seventh floor (men's shoes), only to find a guy with a pencil-thin mustache in a tuxedo playing a grand piano.

The lady in the wheelchair had put me in a bad mood and I felt like causing problems. I lit up a cigarette, ignoring the over 200 "No Smoking! That means you!!" signs hanging at regular intervals along the walls (Actually, all of San Francisco is a no-smoking-area. Another story, but I heard that the Congress is considering to pass a law that would make smoking in your own home illegal) and walked over to this somehow familiar looking Las Vegas invader.

"Hey, dude. You know any Black Flag?"

He looked up at me, still playing. I noticed that his eyes were of two different colors, blue and yellow/green.

"Yeah," he said and proceeded to play a pretty good version of "Revenge" on his piano. So good in fact, that I instantly felt compelled to "piano-dive" – which I did ...

After the smoke had cleared I asked the pianoman, who seemed to be crying, where he had learned to do that on a baby grand, now just a pile of smoldering wood and ivory in front of us.

He blew his nose on his tux and sat down on the floor.

"I ... I used to play bass in Black Flag ..." he stuttered, and then got down to serious sobbing in front of thc bluc sucde "Hush Puppy" shoe display.

"I don't know what happened," he whined, "everything was fine! Anarchy! Booze!! Women ...! And then Henry started singing!!"

By now he was starting to lose control and I was starting to get nervous. In America crying in public is a good way to get arrested – or shot. Losers aren't welcome, and any sign of weakness is routinely dealt with by a show of force. Hell, for all I knew he may well have played for the Flag – but if he did, that was a long time ago, and this blubbering fool on his knees in front of me was starting to attract the attention of the security ... maybe I could help him.

I took one of the shoes he was crying into and whacked him on the side of his head with it.

"Get up, you parasite," I said, "do you want to spend the rest of your life pissing blood in the basement of Alcatraz?!"

He grabbed my leg and started crying harder.

"It wasn't my fault!! It was Heeenry!!!"

No hope. I hit him with the shoe again and then signalled to the security to come and clean the mess up.

"He says he works for Castro," I told the first uniform I saw, "He was trying to sell me cigars."

I escaped to the sounds of his cries for mercy. I had very little sympathy. Just another bum who "coulda been somebody", but wasn't.

I reached the elevators, got down to street level and decided to go back to my hotel and relax with CNN for a while.

On my way back I got stopped by a young punk girl begging for money. "You got twenty bucks so I can buy a gun and kill all these dumb motherfuckers?" she begged, motioning with her hand in front of her.

"Which dumb motherfuckers?" I asked.

She looked at me without smiling.

"All of them."

I gave her a fifty dollar bill and wished her luck.

Somewhere behind me I heard a guy screaming: "I am what I am and I'm going to be the very best of what I am! Imitation is nothing more than suicide!" Amen.

Back in my hotel room, I opened a beer, cut some limes, turned on the TV and watched "World Sport" until I fell asleep to the sound of Michael Jordan explaining that although the Bulls had won again, he still wasn't feeling in top form ...

Fourty points a game just isn't enough. In America "good" is nothing. Only greatness is tolerated. Anything else is second page news ...

I spent many weeks in San Francisco (and, later, Oakland – what a godforsaken city that is) and had many adventures, too many to go into here, but I'll tell you this: As I was experiencing America just before the turn of the century, as I was watching an old man die of a heart-attack on the floor of McDonalds, as I wrestled with whether or not to kill Tom Petty, during many conversations with many important (and some not so important) people – I often found myself preoccupied, and sometimes downright distracted by ... well, by distractions, you know? Hell, I'm easily distracted. Who cares anyway? I had a job to do and I did it. End of story.

And what happened after the job was finished? I took my last three Taxilan, tossed the elephant rifle in an airport dumpster, got on a plane ...

And flew home.

Tour Diary (XI)

22. October, Bielefeld (25)

Okay, bad news first. My 3rd reading here and I always get fewer people than the time before (70, 40 and now 25 – is somebody trying to tell me something?). Sure, it's not a huge disaster, but it is irritating. Anyway, Jan stayed home with a serious toothache, so I had to read alone. 1 1/2 hours, and I was good. Had to deal with some "Jesus Freak" chick who was obviously on some kind of powerful narcotic. I tried to be nice but she didn't make it easy on me. We discussed the relevance of God in a modern society, and then I told her that I thought Satan was groovey. Almost felt guilty as they were throwing her out, but not really. It was a fun evening.

Desperate Letter (II)

Re: Stay in Germany, get rich & famous – or go back to America and live on the streets ...

Okay, I went to the "Ausländer Amt", and it looks like this:

1. I lied to you. I am legal here until 30.06.97, not 30.04.97 like I said. I have to wait until June before they'll give me a new stamp in my pass. Good news, actually.

2. I have to have some control of the German language. Believe it or not, this is no problem. I already dazzled the fucker this morning with my use of complicated sentences and words.

3. I have to have health insurance. Once again – no problem – I hope. As you read this I'll be sitting with a friend of mine (Jesus) who's helping me to fill out the Fragebogen for the KÜNSTLERSOZIALKASSE. To tell the truth, it would surprise me if I wasn't accepted. I am, after all, a true artist. If you know anybody, however, who's already done this and might have some tips on the best way to

fill these things, then I am open for every suggestion.

4. Now the important part: They have to believe that, as long as I live in Germany, I will be making enough money to live from. I told the guy that I will be signing a record contract for 4 records over the next few years and that there is money to be made. I think he might have even believed me. The way I see it, there are three possibilities:

A) "Worse Case" Scenario: I go back to the Ausländer-people in June. I take a copy of the Semaphore contract with me and anything official-looking I can get from Jens. I also tell them that I work in a kneipe, which is true. They tell me it's not enough and kick me out of the country. I go back to America, start working at McDonald's and eventually murder my father 'cause he's a Nazi motherfucker. I rot in prison 'til I die. Not pretty ...

B) "Could be better" Scenario: I take the Semaphore contract, whatever I can get from Jens, the kneipe job and a so-called "fake" job (Somebody signs a real contract saying that, yes, Lee Hollis does work for me – uh, let's say – part-time. Only it's a lie. I don't know the details involved but I think it's possible.). The ausländer people believe me and let me stay in the country.

Fine, except for the fact that the job is fake. Paying rent becomes an obsession with me. I start taking even more drugs than I do now because I can't handle the fact that I'm a loser with no money. I overdose in some dirty backstage room in East Germany and die a painful, embarrassing death. Auch nicht so toll ...

C) "We will rule the fucking world" Scenario: The same as "B", but the job is real. I know this works because I had the same situation with X-Mist Records. I had a part-time job (working for X-Mist) that kept me legal, mentally stable (I think the minimum is something like 500 marks a month) and gave me the flexibility of being able to, for example, go on tour for a few months without having to worry about whether I would have a place to live or not when I got back. Spermbirds became a legend and opened the door for Steak Knife ... and here I am.

If none of that works then Mirja and I get married and live on some remote island in the Caribbean. Auch cool – but does she cook? I don't. That's all the info I have at the moment. I don't think the situation is that desperate at the moment. The bottom line, however, is: Come June, these people have to believe that I'm making enough "regalmazig" money to take care of myself as long as I'm in the country. And who knows? Maybe by that time it will be true. I do know that something has to happen and that I take this very, very seriously. Enough.

Tour Diary (XII)

23. October, Braunschweig (looked like 30)

Lesung – good. Women – beautiful. Alcohol, drugs, excess. Too much, and once again I pay the price. Can't go on like this. Need to get home ...

24. October, Hamburg (60)

Simply put: Great. Possibly one of the best on the tour. Met Schildy for the first time in almost two years. He told me that cutting down trees in Canada is more fun than beating up drunken perverts at the S&M bar he used to work at. I'm not sure that I believe him. Ah hell, it was just a cool evening, and if Bingen is half as good as last night then I can go home a satisfied man. And hey, I haven't puked all day ...

I stopped writing after that. Bingen was cool and I got paid, so I didn't have to hurt anybody. Soon I'll be coming to your town. (CENSORED)

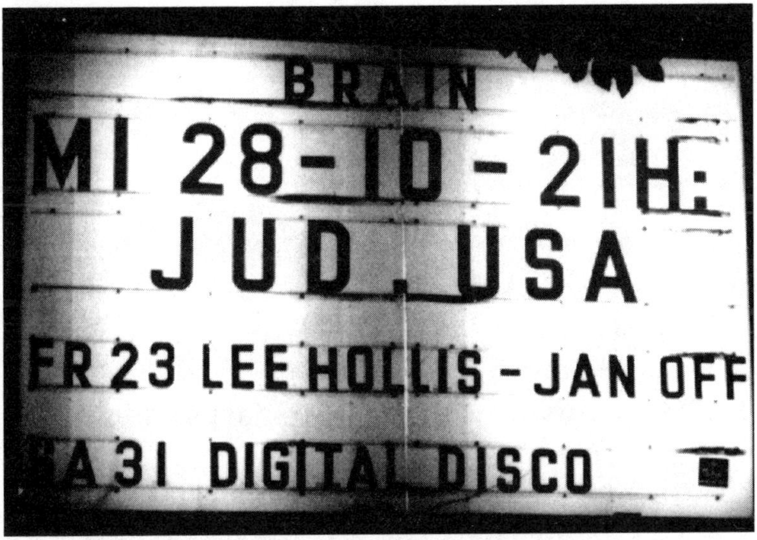
BRAIN
MI 28-10-21H:
JUD USA
FR 23 LEE HOLLIS - JAN OFF
SA 31 DIGITAL DISCO

McDonalds As A Way Of Life

(So you want to be an American?)

1. Smile.
2. Keep smiling.
3. Make friends with strangers fast and forget them even faster.
4. Throw your president out of office because he's gettin' some and you're probably not.
5. Glorify violence and fear sex.
6. Leave the television on when you leave the house.
7. Ah hell, just leave the TV on all the time.
8. Pray to technology.
9. Forget what we did to the Indians.
10. Have a nice day!

Der Autor

Spoken-Words-Performance heißt das aktuelle Zauberwort, und **Lee Hollis** ist der Mann der Stunde. Über die „Ochsen-Tour“ (fast 150 Lesungen in drei Jahren) eroberte er die Herzen der ZuhörerInnen. Seine Stories sind voller Witz, Charme und Selbstironie. Bei seinen Spoken-Words-Performances spielt er seine Entertainerqualitäten voll aus.

Als GI nach Deutschland gekommen, avancierte **Lee Hollis** ab Mitte der 80er Jahre zu dem bedeutendsten Sänger und Texter in der deutschen Hardcore- und Punk-Szene. Er ist der mitreissende Frontmann von Bands wie Steakknife und den Spermbirds.